30p

WHATEVER WANDA WANTED

To **Luther, Jack and Daisy** – GROUP HUG!!
and with special thanks to **Shena**
for her contribution to this story
J.W.

First published in 2001 in Great Britain by

GULLANE
CHILDREN'S BOOKS

Winchester House, 259-269 Old Marylebone Road,
London NW1 5XJ

2 3 4 5 6 7 8 9 10

Text and illustrations © Jude Wisdom 2001
The right of Jude Wisdom to be identified as the author
and illustrator of this work has been asserted by her in
accordance with the Copyright, Designs, and Patents Act, 1988.

A CIP record for this title is available from the British Library.

ISBN 1-86233-215-0 hardback
ISBN 1-86233-300-9 paperback

Printed and bound in Hong Kong

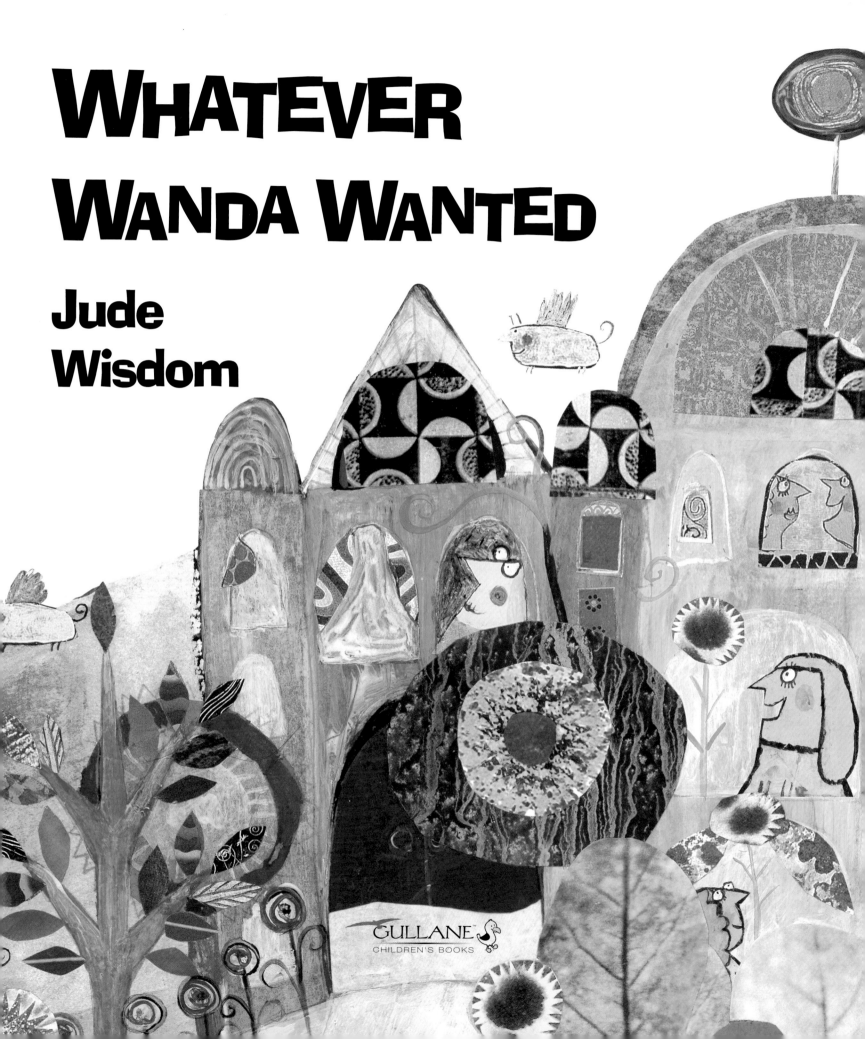

WHATEVER WANDA WANTED

Jude Wisdom

GULLANE
CHILDREN'S BOOKS

Wanda's mum and dad were
very busy people. They decided that
because there wasn't much time to spare,
they would buy little Wanda everything
she could ever want - just to show
how much they cared.

The cutest doll, the frilliest frock, the prettiest kitten – Wanda only had to stamp her tiny foot and it was hers. Year by year, the gifts grew greater. Life-sized dolls, pond-sized paddling pools, cinema-sized tellies – the house was stuffed with presents. Because whatever Wanda wanted, Wanda got!

At school, Wanda had the biggest and best
lunch box of all, but if she spotted
something in someone else's box
she wanted, she'd stamp and
scream until she got that too.

And if one of her classmates brought in
a new toy at 'show-and-tell', Wanda would
reply, "Oh, I've got twenty-three of those."
So, as you can imagine, the one thing
Wanda didn't have was any friends.

One day, Wanda and her mum
headed for the shops as usual.
"I want an ice cream," wailed
Wanda, as soon as they got there.
"Certainly darling, won't be
a tick," said her mum and
she rushed off to buy one.

Mr Yum yum

Wanda waited impatiently. Then, out of the corner of her eye, she spotted a shop she had never seen before – and Wanda had seen all the shops!

As Wanda stepped inside,
she gasped in amazement.
Hanging from the ceiling were hundreds of
kites – kites of every shape and every colour.
But there was one that really caught Wanda's eye.

Hanging from the ceiling was
a magnificent kite, a truly tremendous kite,
the biggest and best kite of them all!

"Can I help you?" asked the shopkeeper.
"I want that kite," snapped Wanda.
"Ah yes, beautiful isn't it. But that
particular kite is not for sale."

"Give me the kite,"
hissed Wanda.

"Not for sale,"
said the
shopkeeper.

Well, that did it. Wanda glared, Wanda stamped,
Wanda spluttered and her face turned red
with fury. She ranted and raged until
her eyes became as big as dustbin lids . . .
"I WANT THAT KITE! I WANT IT NOW!" she screamed.
"ALL RIGHT!" yelled the shopkeeper,
"Have it, but beware Wanda . . .

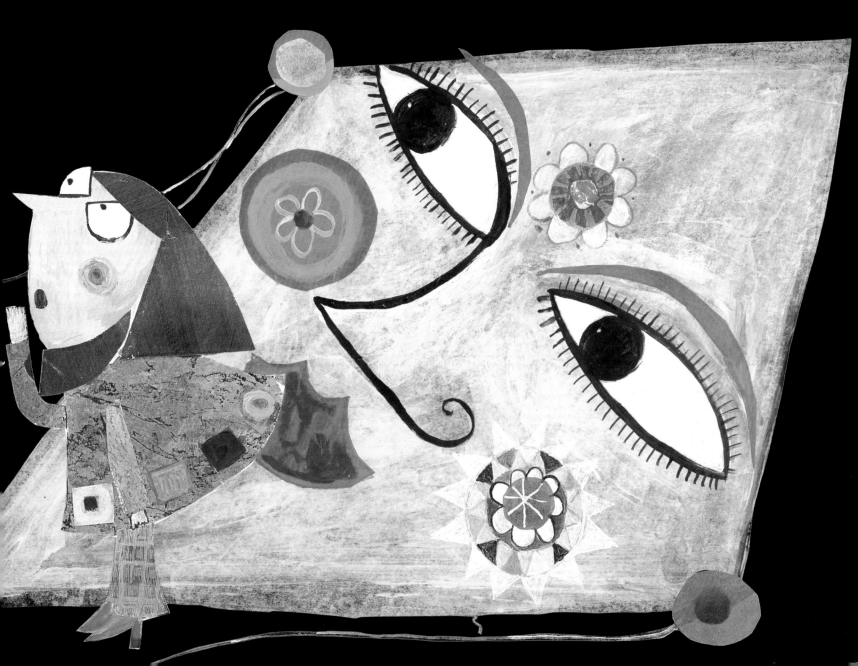

The kite that you choose is a wonderful sight,
A marvellous, magical, mystical kite,
A truly remarkable kite, but beware,
It can do horrid things when it's up in the air!"

But Wanda wasn't listening.
She had grabbed hold of
the kite's silvery string.
"GOT YOU, KITE!" she said . . .

"GOT YOU, WANDA!" said the kite, and before Wanda knew it,
she was being whisked through the door,
up and up, away into the sky.

"Wanda, where are you gooooing?" called her mum, as Wanda flew past.

Wanda held on for dear life
as they soared over the town.
On they flew over fields and
mountains and tiny villages,
until they reached the ocean.

"Time you learnt a few lessons,"
said the kite with a sharp little flick
of its string, and Wanda found
herself tumbling downwards.

Wanda landed with a thump on a tiny desert island. "I'm stranded," she wailed. "What am I going to do? Where are my toys and my clothes and who will cook my breakfast, and . . ." she bit her lip and her eyes filled with tears, ". . . THERE'S NO TELLY!" Things had never looked worse for Wanda.

But, as the sun warmed Wanda's face and dried her tears, she began to feel a little better. "I WILL SURVIVE!" she shouted to a surprised seagull. And that is exactly what she did.

She built a hut from bamboo sticks and made herself a skirt from banana leaves. She made bowls, saucepans and spoons from coconut shells.
Then she built a fire and made some seaweed soup for lunch.

As the days went by, Wanda grew to love her new life. One day, a passing whale called Bill smelt Wanda's delicious fish stew and decided to drop in for a chat. Wanda invited him to stay for dinner.

Wanda and Bill soon became firm friends.
Every evening, Bill would drop by to sample
one of Wanda's wonderful meals. They chatted
and told jokes and looked up at the twinkling stars.

"You know, Bill," said Wanda one evening. "I don't
miss my fancy frocks, or the telly, or any of my toys.
I just really, really, miss my mum and dad."
And a large salty tear fell from Wanda's eye
and landed, plop!, in the seaweed soup.

"But Wanda, why didn't you say?" cried Bill.
"Hop on my back and I'll have you home in no time!"

One week later, Wanda and Bill sailed into town.
Wanda's mum and dad were overjoyed to see her.

"We've searched far and wide for you!" said Dad. "We had to sell your toys, the furniture, even the house."

"And the dishwasher!" said Mum, glumly.

"Don't worry," said Wanda, "I'll soon knock us up some new furniture —

Stick with me and you'll be fine!
You'll see, we'll live like kings
And I've decided anyway . . .

The ~~End~~
The Beginning!